BARBARA HELEN BERGER

A Lot of Otters

PUFFIN BOOKS

Mother Moon
was looking for her child.
"Where is my moonlet?
Where is—"

Oops.

Mother Moon
was looking for her child.
"Where is my moonlet?
Where is my little one?"

She called and called.
She cried and cried.
With every tear
that fell from her eyes,
a star fell into the sea.

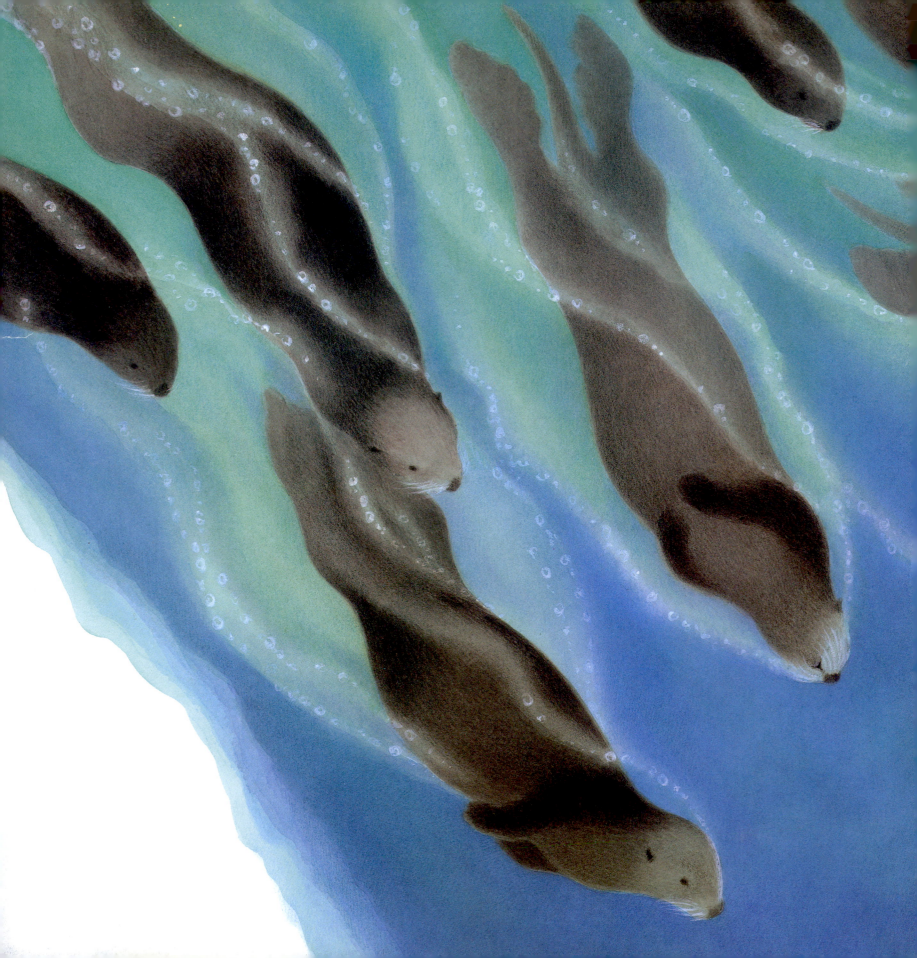

A lot of otters
saw the stars fall.
They dove down
into the dark,

down into the deep.

They carried the stars
up to the top of the sea.

The otters tasted the stars.

They wrestled and rolled
and rubbed the starlight
into their fur.

They bobbed and cavorted
and rollicked around.
They made
such a commotion of light
that Mother Moon
looked down.

"Moonlet? My little one?"
She came running out of the clouds,
over the dark, over the deep.

There
she found her child,
safe with a lot of otters

in a sea of stars.

To Pat

PUFFIN BOOKS
Published by the Penguin Group
Penguin Putnam Books for Young Readers, 345 Hudson Street, New York, New York 10014, U.S.A.
Penguin Books Ltd, 27 Wrights Lane, London W8 5TZ, England
Penguin Books Australia Ltd, Ringwood, Victoria, Australia
Penguin Books Canada Ltd, 10 Alcorn Avenue, Toronto, Ontario, Canada M4V 3B2
Penguin Books (N.Z.) Ltd, 182-190 Wairau Road, Auckland 10, New Zealand

Penguin Books Ltd, Registered Offices: Harmondsworth, Middlesex, England

First published in the United States of America by Philomel Books, 1997
Published by Puffin Books, a division of Penguin Putnam Books for Young Readers, 2000

9 10 8

THE LIBRARY OF CONGRESS HAS CATALOGED THE PHILOMEL EDITION AS FOLLOWS:
Berger, Barbara. A lot of otters / Barbara Helen Berger.
p. cm.
Summary: As a lot of otters wrestle, roll, and cavort on the water, they make such
a commotion of light that Mother Moon finds her lost child.
[1. Lost children—Fiction. 2. Otters—Fiction. 3. Moon—Fiction.] I. Title.
PZ7.B4513Lo 1997 [E]—DC20 95-50532 CIP AC
ISBN 0-399-22910-8

Puffin Books ISBN 978-0-698-11863-8

Manufactured in China
Set in Garamond Light